E
Hu

Hutchins, Pat
The surprise party.

DATE DUE

JE 16 '87	SE 21 '90	AG 5 '93	MY 30 '01
JY 28 '87	NO 23 '90	MAY 28 '94	DE 13 '08
AG 18 '87	DE 15 '90	MAR 25 '95	MY 07 '15
SE 11 '87	MR 7 '91	DEC 14 '95	JY 15 '15
NO 11 '87	AG 5 '91	MAR 26 '96	JY 12 '18
FE 8 '88	AG 24 '91	MAY 02 '96	
MY 15 '89	SE 17 '91	JUN 19	
JE 14 '89	NO 7 '91	JE 26 '00	
JY 26 '89	AP 2 '92	SE 20 '00	
AG 14 '89	JY 16 '92	AP 12 '01	
AG 14 '89	AG 7 '92	JE 26 '01	
JY 26 '90	NO 19 '92	JY 13 '01	

—DEMCO—

THE SURPRISE PARTY

PAT HUTCHINS

THE SURPRISE PARTY

MACMILLAN PUBLISHING COMPANY   NEW YORK

Macmillan Publishing Company, 866 Third Avenue, New York, NY 10022
Collier Macmillan Canada, Inc.
First published 1969; reissued 1986.
Printed in the United States of America

10 9 8 7 6 5 4 3 2 1

Library of Congress Cataloging-in-Publication Data • Hutchins, Pat, date.
The surprise party. Summary: Rabbit confides to Owl that he is planning a
party, but as the message is passed from animal to animal it gets more and
more confused.
[1. Animals—Fiction. 2. Communication—Fiction] I. Title.
PZ7.H96165Su   1986   [E]   86-7255   ISBN 0-02-745930-6

for MORGAN

"I'm having a party tomorrow," whispered Rabbit.
"It's a surprise."

"Rabbit is hoeing the parsley tomorrow," whispered Owl.
"It's a surprise."

"Rabbit is going to sea tomorrow," whispered Squirrel.
"It's a surprise."

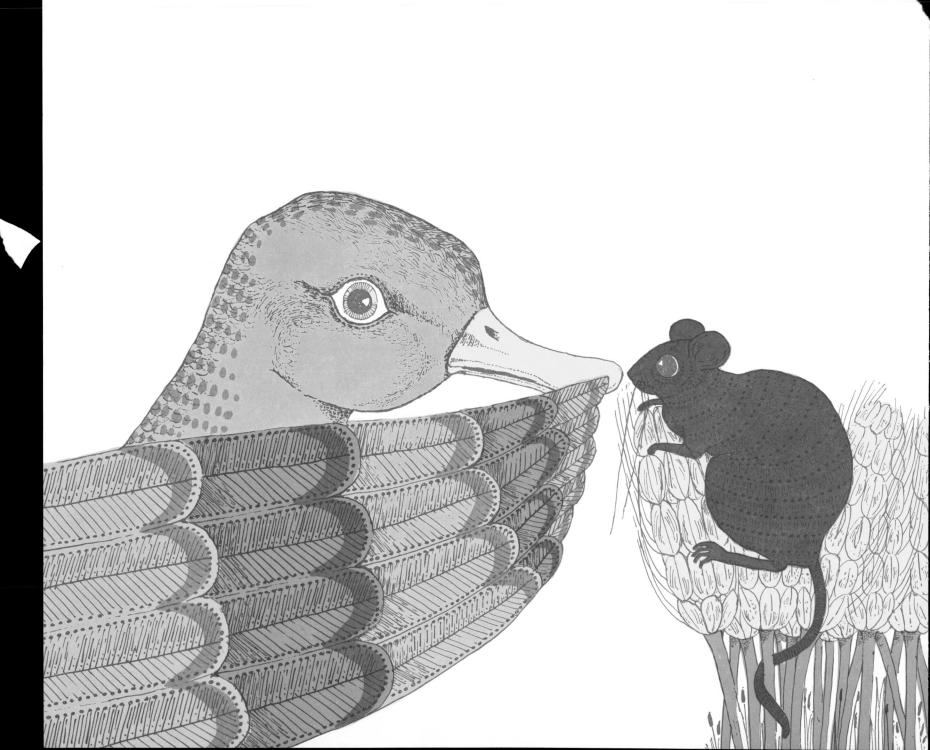

"Rabbit is climbing a tree tomorrow," whispered Duck.
"It's a surprise."

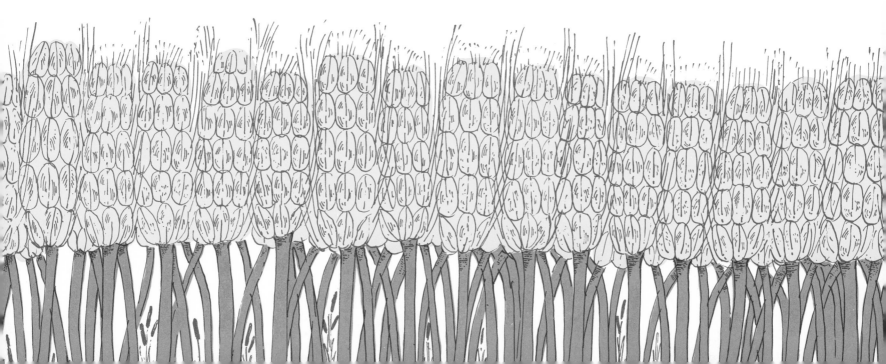

"Rabbit is riding a flea tomorrow," whispered Mouse.
"It's a surprise."

"Rabbit is raiding the poultry tomorrow," whispered Fox.
"It's a surprise."

"Reading poetry?" said Frog to himself.
"His own, I suppose. How dull."

The next day Rabbit went to see Frog.

"Come with me, Frog," he said.

"I have a surprise for you."

"No, thank you," said Frog.

"I know your poetry. It puts me to sleep."

And he hopped away.

So Rabbit went to see Fox.
"Come with me, Fox," he said.
"I have a surprise for you."

"No, thank you," said Fox.
"I don't want you raiding the poultry.
I'll get the blame."
And he ran off.

So Rabbit went to see Mouse.

"Come with me, Mouse," he said.

"I have a surprise for you."

"No, thank you," said Mouse.
"A rabbit riding a flea?
Even I am too big for that."
And Mouse scampered away.

So Rabbit went to see Duck.
"Come with me, Duck," he said.
"I have a surprise for you."

"No, thank you," said Duck.
"Squirrel told me you were climbing a tree.
Really, you're too old for that sort of thing."
And Duck waddled off.

So Rabbit went to see Squirrel.

"Come with me, Squirrel," he said.

"I have a surprise for you."

"No, thank you," said Squirrel.
"I know you're going to sea,
but good-byes make me sad."
And Squirrel ran up the tree.

So Rabbit went to see Owl.

"Owl," he said, "I don't know what YOU think I'm doing, but

I'M HAVING A PARTY."

And this time everyone heard clearly.

"A party!" they shouted. "Why didn't you say so?"
"A party! How nice!"

And it was a nice party.

And such a surprise.